MARVEL

A BLACK PANTHER ADVENTURE

SHURI

HEAT

#2

WILKERSON 19

NIC STONE

is the *New York Times* bestselling author of the novels *Dear Martin* and *Odd One Out*. She was born and raised in a suburb of Atlanta, Georgia, and the only thing she loves more than an adventure is a good story about one. After graduating from Spelman College, she worked extensively in teen mentoring and lived in Israel for a few years before returning to the United States to write full-time. Having grown up with a wide range of cultures, religions, and backgrounds, she strives to bring diverse voices and stories into her work. Learn more at nicstone.info.

SHURI

BY **NIC STONE**

SCHOLASTIC INC.

ABDOBOOKS.COM

Reinforced library bound edition published in 2021 by Spotlight, a division of ABDO, PO Box 398166, Minneapolis, Minnesota 55439. Spotlight produces high-quality reinforced library bound editions for schools and libraries. Reprinted by permission of Scholastic Inc.

Printed in the United States of America, North Mankato, Minnesota.
092020
012021

THIS BOOK CONTAINS
RECYCLED MATERIALS

© 2020 MARVEL

First printing 2020

Book design by Katie Fitch

Library of Congress Control Number: 2020942435

Publisher's Cataloging-in-Publication Data

Names: Stone, Nic, author.
Title: Heat / by Nic Stone.
Description: Minneapolis, Minnesota : Spotlight, 2021. | Series: Shuri: a Black Panther adventure; #2
Summary: Shuri thinks sneaking out of the palace with K'Marah will be the most difficult part of her mission, but when they leave Wakanda, the girls discover that not everyone feels the same way about Wakanda.
Identifiers: ISBN 9781532147746 (lib. bdg.)
Subjects: LCSH: Shuri (Fictitious character)--Juvenile fiction. | Wakanda (Africa : Imaginary place)--Juvenile fiction. | Princesses--Juvenile fiction. | Escapes--Juvenile fiction. | Adventure and adventurers--Juvenile fiction. | Black Panther (Fictitious character)--Juvenile fiction | Graphic novels--Juvenile fiction
Classification: DDC [Fic]--dc23

Spotlight
A Division of ABDO
abdobooks.com

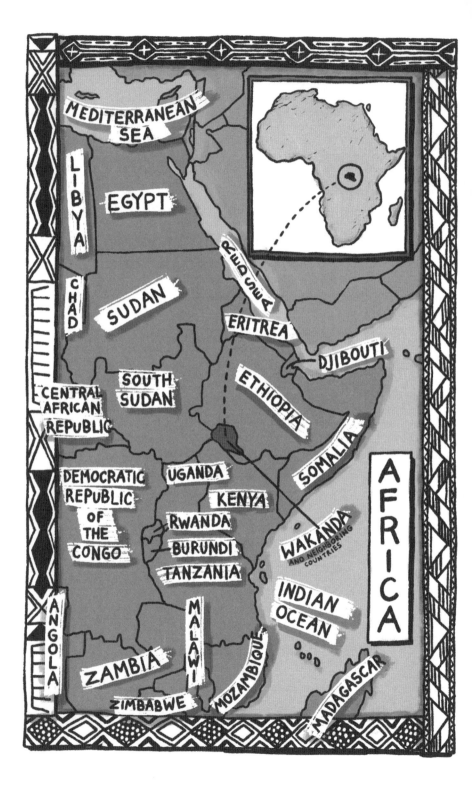

6

PRINCESS PROBLEM SOLVER

Together.

Tuh.

Explains why Shuri's standing in the throne room *alone* while T'Challa zips off to handle matters she's clearly being excluded from, right?

She literally stomps—though it makes no sound because her feet are clad in sound-absorbing, Vibranium-soled slippers. Another of her inventions.

Why do he and Mother insist on treating her like some melodramatic child? It's clear that Mother finds the notion of a priest keeping a secret unfathomable.

(Does she also believe the Dora Milaje tell her *every-thing*?) But T'Challa? Shuri expected better from him.

But fine: Since they're both preoccupied, Shuri will take care of it herself. Bast help her, *within* the hyper-limited pre-Challenge time frame. And in doing so, she will prove to Mother and T'Challa—to *everyone*, really—that she's more than just some princess history will forget.

She exits the throne room with what feels like sacred fire crackling in her bone marrow, formulating a plan as her feet pad soundlessly over the marble floors. From what she's deduced so far, something is destroying the plant cells from the inside. Which seems like a simple problem to solve: Isolate the foreign agent, figure out how it's getting in, and find a way to eliminate it.

But it hasn't been simple at all. And after watching T'Challa's vessel shoot toward the storm cloud–filled horizon, Shuri gets a flash of an idea, not unlike the brilliant strike of lightning in the distance, that she hopes will get her one step closer to figuring out *why*.

What every Wakandan primary schooler knows: Thousands of years ago a meteorite made of Vibranium crashed to Earth, creating the Sacred Mound that, to this day, is mined by members of K'Marah's home tribe for the highly valuable substance. Civilization eventually sprang up around it, and now Wakanda, secret bastion of science and technology, exists as one of the most advanced nations in the world.

And something *Shuri* knows as a member of the royal family and descendant of Bashenga, the first-ever Black Panther: The heart-shaped herb's panther-prowess-giving properties come from a Vibranium-rooted mutation that permanently altered the composition of the plant.

But there's more. Something that *hadn't* occurred to her until that jagged shoot of electricity in the sky jogged her memory.

Three years ago, while working on a project for her History of the Wakandas course with a professor so mystical in his leanings that Shuri had a tendency to write off just about everything he said, she stumbled upon the digital archive of an ancient text. Like, words-hand-printed-on-what-looked-like-pages-made-from-the-papery-casing-that-protects-the-pulp-of-the-baobab-fruit type of ancient.

At the time, she chalked the reading up to myth, but now, a piece of it pulses at the front edge of her consciousness, almost like it's radioactive: According to the parchment, ancient Wakandans figured out how to manipulate storm clouds in a way that channeled celestial energies. This—supposedly—created the pathway that pulled the Wakandan Vibranium meteorite down to Earth.

As the princess practically skips back to her chambers, a series of mildly unscientific ideas begin to coalesce in her head. She'll have to leave Wakanda to get to the source of the information she's after . . . but if there's a chance of saving the herb—and her own potential future by extension—it's worth both the risk and extra effort.

Shuri carefully closes her door and rushes into her closet to begin making calculations and gathering supplies.

A check of her Kimoyo card reveals that there are precisely three days, six hours, twenty-seven minutes, and forty-four . . . forty-three, forty-two, forty-one, forty . . . seconds until the Challenge will commence.

Once inside her own travel vessel, Shuri will need approximately eighty-six minutes to reach her destination. Hopefully, it won't take long to make contact with her . . . contact. The princess will explain the dilemma and ask her questions, then get on her way back home with the right answers—or at least some new information that will help lead her in the right direction.

She can depart in the morning and return within twenty-four hours. Which will leave her with just over two days to complete a version of the Panther Habit that will get T'Challa through Challenge Day minimally scathed and with maximum flexibility, and if not *solve* the issue with the herb, at least deduce what is causing it.

So absorbed is the princess in her planning, she doesn't realize she has a visitor until a voice rings out from behind her.

"I take it your conversation with the king was fruitful?"

Shuri, who is kneeling to gather a few items from beneath the normally hidden lab station, startles and pops up too quickly, smacking the back of her head against the underside of the slide-out table.

"OW!" Rubbing the forming knot, she turns to find the queen mother now looking past her at the no-longer-secret science sanctuary.

"What in the name of—"

"The conversation went great, Mother!" Shuri says, closing the space between herself and the queen, then grabbing her mother's hand to pull her out into the open space of the bedroom. "Let me tell you *all* about it."

Queen Ramonda allows herself to be led to the bed, but when Shuri sits and pats the open space beside her—"Join me!" *Smile for effect*—Mother refuses to take the bait.

Crosses her arms instead. "What are you up to, child? And *what* is that . . . contraption inside your dressing chamber?"

"That old thing?" Shuri makes her best attempt at a dismissive wave. "Nothing at all! A small . . . experimentation-site-sort-of thing I built for those early-morning *Eureka!* moments. You know how fleeting they can be. T'Challa sends his regards!"

The queen's eyes narrow, and then she cocks her head to one side and a slight grin tugs at the corners of her mouth.

This is when Shuri knows she's in trouble.

"And where are you going, Daughter?"

A miniature big bang occurs at the base of Shuri's throat, creating a universe of panic she can't seem to speak beyond. She swallows in an attempt to force it down, which only serves to create a spinning, churning sensation in her stomach.

She does manage to hold the gas in this time. "Hmm?"

"The open carry case on your dressing chamber floor you were filling with different items when I came in. Are you planning a trip somewhere?"

"Just to my lab!" Shuri practically shouts, so excited by the validity of the lie, she can hardly contain herself. "I brought those vials and flasks here last week while working on a trial I needed to monitor over-night. I know how you feel about my staying in the lab past curfew. Just trying to fulfill your wishes, Mother."

"Mm-hmm. And the change of clothes I saw?"

Geesh, the woman has the eyesight of an African hawk eagle. "Those are for, uhh . . . in case I spill something! I read somewhere that working in clean clothes is good for productivity. Cleanliness is next to Bastliness, you know!"

"Cleanliness is next to—?" The queen mother shakes her head, but Shuri can see that her blathering is working. "What am I going to do with you, Shuri?"

"Trust me more," the princess says as she rises to gently usher her mother to the door.

"I *trust* that T'Challa impressed upon you the importance of keeping us abreast of your movements?"

"Absolutely," Shuri replies. "One-hundred-and-fifty percent, Mother." *Almost there.* "If I move, there will be a full announcement over the intra-palace communication network."

The queen turns to glare at her. "Do not patronize me, child."

Whoops! Too far.

Thankfully, they're at the door now.

"I think I'm going to call it a night!" Shuri opens her mouth wide in a fake yawn. "Thanks for coming by to check on me, Mumsie!"

The queen mother steps into the hall, and the two Dora Milaje guards posted outside the princess's chambers fall into formation at the queen's sides, ready to escort her to wherever she's headed next.

As they walk away, Shuri exhales.

But then Mother stops.

"Shuri," she calls without turning around.

The princess shuts her eyes. "Yes, Mother?"

"I have your word that you will permit at least one guard to escort you to your laboratory?"

Fabulous. "Yes, Mother."

"Excellent. I will alert General Okoye of your intentions to make the journey. I am *trusting* you to be in contact with her with the details of *precisely* when. Am I understood?"

Shuri sighs. "Yes, ma'am."

The queen gives a curt nod and continues up the hall, away from her daughter and the smoldering wreckage that is Shuri's Save-the-Nation-in-Three-Days-or-Less plan.

Once Mother and her pair of (*unnecessary*, considering they're inside the most fortified edifice in Wakanda) warrior companions disappear around a corner, Shuri turns around, slumps back against her gilded bedroom wall, and slides to the floor like low-viscosity silicone oil down the side of a glass vial.

Except this time when she closes her eyes, she sees the globe of her homeland crushed to dust, and hears an echo of one of the words she heard near the fire: *khusela.*

Protect.

In fact, if she didn't know better, she'd swear someone is whispering it into her ear.

Her eyes snap open, but this time, instead of panic, Shuri feels only the prickling sizzle of determination ghost over her skin.

She lifts her arms, shifts her Kimoyo beads, and taps to call her dear brother.

7

PANTHER

And . . . T'Challa doesn't answer. (Typical.)

Which leaves Shuri with no choice but to camp outside his quarters until he returns from wherever he zipped off to.

It's after ten p.m. when he finally does. He's still in his Panther suit, but without the mask. And he appears weary.

He's also clearly *not* expecting to find his little sister waiting outside his door, looking like she has lit charcoal powder coursing beneath her skin.

He stops dead when he sees her. Then shakes his

head. "I should have known you would be here," he says, nodding at the two Dora Milaje standing sentinels in turn. He pushes the door open, and as Shuri follows him into the vast space beyond, she notices his slightly wonky gait, and how the habit he's wearing . . . rides up in the back.

Looks quite uncomfortable.

So there's no turning back.

"I need your help," she says, pushing past the urge to ask why his shoulders are slumped and what's happening at the border and why it took so long for him to return and if they're going to be invaded. It's not as though he would actually *answer* any of those queries.

"We are not postponing Challenge Day, Shuri. Herb problem or no herb problem, it is completely out of the question—"

"That's not what I mean."

Now he turns to look at her.

Shuri takes a deep breath. "I need you to cover for me, T'Challa."

He crosses his arms. "Cover for you."

"Yes."

"While you do *what*, exactly?"

On the walk over from her own rooms, Shuri decided she'd lean into the lie she'd told Mother: She wants to spend some uninterrupted time in her lab.

She's hoping that because T'Challa gave her the suit task, and she has to be in the lab to complete it, he'll do as she asks and tell Mother there's no need for her "guards."

"I mean, nothing *too* terrible or risky. Just want to work on your suit. That wedgie looks . . ." She cringes for effect. "Yikes."

T'Challa scowls. "Why do you need a cover?"

"Wellll . . . after learning of my visit to the Sacred Field, Mother is watching me more closely. If she had her way, I'd be consistently surrounded by her informants so she can keep minutely detailed tabs on my every movement."

Now T'Challa smirks. "Not too terrible an idea, if you ask me."

Shuri rolls her eyes. "So you'll do it, then? I need freedom to work from approximately zero eight hundred hours into the evening."

He shakes his head. "You know how Mother is, Shuri. I'll request that the guard stay outside the lab so as not to distract you—"

"T'Challa, *please*. The presence of a guard within a one-hundred-meter radius would be distracting. You know how experimentation goes . . . one wrong move triggered by an unexpected sound or motion or *anything*, and KA-BLOOEY! The last thing I need while working on YOUR new habit is some sort of intruder-triggered accident." She throws her hands up.

T'Challa merely raises an eyebrow. "You are not making a good case for your request, Shuri."

The princess sighs. "Are you going to vouch for me or not?"

When he looks away, Shuri knows what his answer will be. "What Mother wants, Mother gets, little sister. You know this as well as I do."

"But she will listen to you, T'Challa! There is no way I can *truly* work with a Dora hovering about, watching my every move! This affects you, too, you know . . ."

"I'm sorry, Shuri. New suit or not, I will not oppose Mother so overtly."

So blackmail it'll be, then.

Shuri lifts her chin. She's not the only one who has slipped into neighboring nations without the queen mother's knowledge. "Cover for me, or I'm going to tell Mother where you were really going on those 'covert scouting missions' last year. *And* the year before. I have video and records of your flight paths." She humphs.

For a moment T'Challa is silent. Then: "So you intend to play hardball, eh?"

The princess lifts her chin higher.

"I must admit, I would not have expected such underhandedness from someone like you, Sister."

"I will do what I must for the good of my country."

At this, T'Challa chuckles. Which ignites a torch of rage within Shuri's chest. This . . . *dismissal* is precisely what she must stand in defiance of. She opens her mouth to respond, but T'Challa speaks again: "Take Ayo," he says. "She can post outside the entrance chamber."

"No way," the princess replies. "Ayo is bound by an oath to the throne. You are the sitting king, and she will do as you say, yes. But as you continue to point out, Mother is the queen. If she did as she said she would and instructed General Okoye to have *all* Dora Milaje report back to her regarding my activities, they are bound to do so, T'Challa. No matter which Dora is sent, I'll be monitored more closely than our Vibranium stores."

T'Challa considers this for a moment, then sighs and lifts his arms. "Sorry, Sis. No guard, no go," he says.

His Kimoyo card chimes, and as he checks it, Shuri glances around his surprisingly sparse quarters. Baba had been more extravagant than T'Challa. Gone is the massive four-poster bed with black chiffon canopy. The long, curved leather couch and gold-legged granite table that sat atop the also-missing (synthetic) panther-pelt rug. The pair of larger-than-life-size, hand-carved, black alabaster panther statues that stood sentinel on each side of the room's double doors.

Even the floor-to-ceiling shelves filled with books are gone. ("Better for them to be in the library instead of here collecting dust for the sake of a look," T'Challa had said. And he hadn't been wrong, but still.)

The difference in the space gives her a chill. She tries not to think about it too much, but Shuri misses her father. She has a hunch Baba wouldn't have been opposed to her learning hand-to-hand combat and gaining proficiency with various weapons. Undergoing the same rigorous study-and-training regimen as T'Challa had.

Especially since she's first in line to the throne.

Perhaps it's wishful thinking, but standing in this room, remembering the way her father would launch her into the air above his head and catch her, how excited he'd get when she'd come to him with something she'd built from the little click-blocks she loved to play with as a child, Shuri is *fully* convinced Baba would be behind her in this.

She has to make *him* proud.

Time to bring out the big guns. "I won't have a Dora stationed outside my lab, T'Challa."

"Then perhaps you won't be spending as much time

there as you'd like. Frankly, there isn't much Mother can do about my past indiscretions, so your threat is without impact, and, therefore, without power."

Shuri locks and loads. "Okay," she says with a shrug. Then aims and . . . fires. "Guess I'll just have to tell Nakia how you *really* feel about her."

T'Challa's eyes go wide. "You wouldn't."

"Oh, I absolutely would. Remember that night you drank a bit too much pineapple wine at Eldress Umbusi's birthday party, and I had to assist you?" Shuri reaches into the pocket of her tunic and produces a single Kimoyo bead, which she drops into her bracelet. The moment she taps it, T'Challa's voice fills the cavernous space. *"She is more beautiful than the baobab plain at sunrise. More delightful than the pulp of a ripe mango. She smells better than—"*

"Okay, okay! Stop it!" T'Challa says, and Shuri smiles as she shuts the bead off.

"Quit your *grinning*," he continues. "You will have six hours."

"*Six?*" That won't work for her *true* plan. At least two would be eaten by travel, and once you add an additional half hour on each end to *prepare* for travel, half of the allotted time is gone. "But that's not enough time!"

He shrugs. "You want more time, take a guard."

"I won't be able to truly focus!"

They fall into silence.

But only for a brief moment. Because then T'Challa's face illuminates like an LED filament light bulb.

And in that instant, Shuri knows precisely what he's going to say.

"No . . ." she begins just as he shouts the exact thing she's hoping he won't:

"K'Marah!"

8

MOBILE

Based on the generic *"K"* response Shuri received on her Kimoyo card when she sent K'Marah a text message asking if she would fill the role of "lab assistant" the following day (*"and wear trousers,"* the message said), she's expecting K'Marah to arrive at their meeting point cool, calm, and collected.

She does *not* expect K'Marah to burst into her quarters *before* sunrise, and squeal like a tickled piglet as she somersaults through the air, and lands perfectly on her back in the bed as if she'd slept that way. She turns her face toward the princess, smiling as though the entire scenario were the most normal thing in the world. "Hi."

"You're not serious," Shuri replies, squeezing her eyes shut in hopes that when she opens them again— at least an hour from now—she will find herself alone and discover that *this* was nothing more than a terrible dream.

But then there's another high-pitched squeal. And her bed begins to shake.

Because K'Marah is pounding her arms and kicking her legs like a jittery pre-primary schooler.

"K'Maraaaaaaaaah!"

"I am so *EXCITED!*" K'Marah practically screams.

"Can you keep it down?" Shuri says, walloping her friend with a pillow. "Let's not wake the entire palace!"

"Okay, okay." K'Marah flips onto her side to face the princess, and props her newly cornrowed-and-beaded head on her hand. "So when do we leave?"

The hairs on Shuri's arms rise to attention. K'Marah couldn't know they're *actually* leaving, could she? "I know for a fact that I instructed you to meet me beneath the Panther effigy at the city gates, in trousers, at eight thirty." She looks K'Marah over. "Not only are you wearing a ridiculously impractical *dress*, it's— Time, please!" Shuri says to the air.

The vaguely robotic reply is instantaneous: "The time is zero six hundred hours and twenty-three minutes."

"Six twenty-three?!" Shuri exclaims, shoving K'Marah's shoulder.

"I'm sorry, I'm sorry!" K'Marah flops onto her back and sighs. "I couldn't sleep! I brought clothes to change into, just wanted to look like myself as I came to your quarters—"

Shuri gasps and grabs K'Marah's arm. "How'd you get into the palace?" She turns her head, wide-eyed. "Were you questioned?" Yes, T'Challa talked Mother out of sending a Dora Milaje with Shuri to the lab, but as far as she knows, there is a leather-clad warrior woman just outside the entrance to her chambers. Raising *any* kind of red flags would be disastrous.

K'Marah shoos the panic away. "I took a transport car and came to stay with Uncle shortly after receiving your message last night. Ayo let me in here."

Shuri doesn't respond to that. Even though she does feel a certain *way* about this pseudo-friend of hers having such easy access to the palace.

The shorter girl leans closer and lowers her voice to a whisper. "So what are we *really* doing?"

Oh boy. "What do you mean?"

"The whole lab thing is a cover, right? If I know anything about you, it's that you prefer to work alone. So if you're asking me to be your 'assistant,' there is definitely something else afoot." She taps Shuri's nose.

Shuri is too stunned to respond.

K'Marah grins and returns to her back. "Whatever it is, I can't *wait!* I figured you'd be awake by now because . . . well, you're *you.* But at any rate, we're both up, yeah? Why not get an earlier start?"

The princess groans and throws an arm over her face, but she's unable to deny K'Marah's logic. Besides, the sooner they leave, the more time to gather information. Hopefully.

"Fine," Shuri says.

And she gets up.

◈◈◈◈

Getting out of the palace earlier than Shuri reported to Mother proves a hair more difficult than Shuri expects. The Ayo part is easy: By the time Mother is awake, and the Dora has told her of the girls' predawn departure "to the lab"—with T'Challa's blessing—they'll be en route to Kenya and it'll be too late for the queen to thwart Shuri's plan.

Slipping past the intensely stoic palace guards, though?

And they do have to *slip* past: While it would take fire, flood, or falling bombs for Ayo to wake the queen, the palace guards would instantly report Shuri's movements. And Mother would have her and K'Marah held until she could storm from her chambers and interrogate Shuri.

No thanks.

"Okay, so the plan . . ." Shuri says to K'Marah as the shorter girl finishes the laborious task of tucking her hair into one of the classic caps the market boys wear. They're in the cloakroom near the delivery entrance to the palace, now dressed in the sand-colored garb of male Merchant apprentices.

"Bast, these clothes are itchy," K'Marah complains.

"No great deed was ever done without discomfort." Shuri cracks open the door to the hallway and peeks out. "As I was saying, we need to disable three guards." She squats to rifle through the purple velvet bag at her feet, pulling out a few items and transferring the rest to a less . . . *conspicuous* bag. One that fits their disguises. "Catch," she says, tossing K'Marah a smoke-colored orb about the size of a yellow passion fruit.

"What is this?" the mini-Dora asks, holding it up for examination.

"That," Shuri replies with a grin, "is phase two." She turns back to the cracked doorway and squats, something held loosely in her hand. "Okay, so the security cameras will be playing looped footage for the next ten minutes. Here's what's going to happen: First, I will release a beetle-bot—"

"A *what*?"

"You'll see. Then you will roll that stink bomb out—"

"Stink bomb?!" K'Marah looks at the thing in her hand like it's grown tentacles.

"Stop interrupting! Those two *should* do the trick, but if not, phase three will take out the electricity on this hallway for approximately four-point-three-two seconds. I'll lead us out with my thermal imaging goggles."

"Thermal imaging gog—you know what, never mind. Let's get this over with."

As K'Marah—and the wildly unprepared guards—come to discover, a beetle-bot is just that: a robot shaped like a giant flower beetle.

When guard two notices the thing crawling up guard one's trouser leg, he screams . . . and then kicks.

"Yikes!" K'Marah says as guard one goes down, the fake bug still making its way up toward the man's head.

"Phase two!" Shuri whisper-shouts. K'Marah depresses the little button on the stink bomb as Shuri instructs. Then quick as she can, she rolls the thing into the hallway.

Shuri instantly shuts the door and yanks one of the cloaks down to stuff beneath it. "It's very potent," she says to K'Marah.

And then there's a *THUD*. The girls look at each other, but neither speaks.

After a few breaths of silence from the other side of the door, Shuri taps one of her Kimoyo beads, and a glowing countdown leaps into the air. "Thirty-three seconds until the air is clear," she mouths to K'Marah, who shrugs and mouths "*What?*" back.

When the time has elapsed, Shuri carefully removes the cloak from beneath the heavy door and hangs it up. Then even *more* slowly pulls the door open. A hazy, shimmering mist coats the air. The girls wave their noses, though the smell has mostly dissipated.

But then they both stop. "Uhhh . . . Shuri?" K'Marah asks as she takes in the scene. Before them lie three dark green heaps. The guards, one of whom has what looks like a palm-size bug perched on his cheek. "What exactly was *in* that thing?"

"Hydrogen and ammonium sulfides with just a pinch of methane . . . basically the fragrance that would come out of a big man who'd eaten spoiled luwombo. Which . . . maybe I overdid the methane?"

She steps over to guard one to remove her mechani-bug from his face, and gives his leg a little shove with the toe of her boot. He's out cold.

"No need for phase three, I guess?" K'Marah says.

The girls glance at each other wide-eyed and then explode into giggles.

"Let's go," Shuri says.

Within ten minutes, the two girls-dressed-as-boys are passing through the city gates.

"Shuri—" K'Marah begins, but the princess cuts her off.

"Shhh!" Shuri hisses, peeking behind them to make sure they aren't being trailed.

No one even looks twice as they each move through the waking city with dingy brown rucksacks full of clothes and supplies slung over one shoulder. While Shuri forced K'Marah to leave behind most of the froufrou foolishness she'd brought to take on the journey—drapey tunics and patterned silk skirts—K'Marah *did* convince Shuri that she should pack one dress, just in case.

They will be interacting with royalty, after all.

After a couple of minutes of silent trekking on the side of a paved road used solely for weekly transports of Vibranium from the mines to the city, K'Marah takes a look around and then turns to Shuri with the light of many suns dancing in her eyes.

"Uhhhh—" the princess begins nervously, but that's all she gets out because K'Marah whoops so loudly, a flock of starlings launches into the air from deep within a field nearby.

"K'Marah!"

"Shuri, we *made it*! Can you believe it? We made it out in broad daylight with everyone moving about the palace! This is next-level!"

And as much as Shuri wants to shush her now-prancing friend again, she also can't help but smile.

They *did* make it out.

"We are rather enterprising, eh?" Shuri says, giving herself a mental pat on the back.

Her joy does not last, however. Not five minutes later, the girls crest the hill that will lead them down to the baobab plain, which they have to cross to reach Shuri's lab just outside the Sacred Mound, and discover that the plain is occupied.

"Whoa!" Shuri says, grabbing K'Marah's rucksack to pull her down so they can't be seen.

Both girls poke their heads up just enough to see the gathering below. T'Challa stands, in full Panther garb, at the head of what looks like some sort of *Taifa Ngao*: *War Council Edition*—instead of the heads of the various tribes, a group of Wakandan generals, as evidenced by the glint of the newly risen sun off their telltale golden sashes, is gathered in a circle. Eleven men, plus Okoye, plus T'Challa. A baker's dozen of warriors including the king.

"What do you think they're talking about?" K'Marah whispers.

A number of terrifying topics a war council would need to discuss flash through Shuri's head, but she manages to spit out something less dire: "My guess would be the impending Challenge Day. Perhaps they are discussing security measures. The plain *is* where the whole thing will take place, so it would make sense to meet there, yes?"

"You tell me, Princess," K'Marah replies.

Just then, T'Challa's head lifts, and Shuri knows for a fact that despite the distance—and the mask—her dear brother is looking into her eyes. It makes her breath stick right beneath the hollow of her throat.

"You know," K'Marah says, "not to be all harbinger of doom, but I get the distinct impression they are *not* discussing Chall—"

"Time to move," Shuri says, refusing to allow full vent of K'Marah's thought into the atmosphere. "We can talk about it later, but for now, we need to get out of here."

◇◇◇◇◇

By the time they reach the mound—after an additional twenty-five minutes trudging largely at a slant around the field—the cloudless sky has become a curse, and both girls are sweating buckets from the sun beaming down on them without mercy.

They both flop to the floor once inside the cave-like entryway to Shuri's lab. "Welcome to my Innovation Domicile," the princess says, her eyes shut and chest heaving.

"This is it?" K'Marah replies. "*This* is your glorious laboratory?"

"Technically this is the mouth of the cavern that *leads* to the ID. It's down there through those doors." Shuri drags her arm into the air to point, then lets it drop.

"Is there water inside?" K'Marah asks.

"Of course."

"Then let's go." K'Marah climbs to her feet and lifts Shuri up, pulling one of the princess's skinny arms across her own shoulders so the pair can walk in tandem. "I'm on the brink of death from thirst."

"That hyperbole feels wildly inappropriate considering the danger of our imminent undertaking."

"Which you still have not told me about . . ."

"We'll get there, I promise."

The girls slog up the uneven rock floor of the nature-carved hallway, and once in front of the real entrance to the lab, Shuri slaps her hand against a palm scanner. K'Marah looks on, agog, as a purple laser light runs from the tops of Shuri's fingertips down to her wrist and back again.

And when the clouded glass doors slide open and a disembodied female voice—which sounds suspiciously similar to the queen mother's—proclaims, "Welcome, Princess Shuri, Ancient Future, Enlightened One, First of Her Name, Heir to the Throne, and Future Black Panther," K'Marah, now fully alert, turns her widened eyes to her best friend.

"Oh really, now?"

"Shut up."

As soon as they're through the doors, K'Marah does just that.

For a moment, at least. "Holy—"

"K'Marah!"

"Sorry, I just . . ." Shuri watches her friend's eyes roam around what amounts to the lab's foyer. One wall is covered in soundproof foam (experimentation with Vibranium often involves loud noise), but all the others are made of the same thick glass as the entry doors. In a curved arc around the space lay three separate test areas where the princess executes her actual experiments.

"Impressed?" Shuri says, reveling in K'Marah's inability to lift her unhinged jaw from the gleaming epoxy-resin floor. They make their way past the smart boards and cabinets filled with bits and bobs, and approach an open, though darkened, doorway. The moment Shuri steps within a foot of the room, a light clicks on inside, revealing a small kitchen.

"I mean, *wow*," K'Marah says. Shuri reaches into a miniature cooler—run on Vibranium, of course—and hands K'Marah a small glass bottle of water. Then she uncaps one for herself, and gulps it down.

After opening a few cabinets and pulling different snacks from within to add to her rucksack—dried hibiscus calyxes and mango slices; rice crackers and a variety of hard cheeses—Shuri turns to a still-stunned K'Marah. "Ready?"

"Uhhh . . . I think so?"

Now the princess can't stop smiling. "Right this way." She heads toward what looks like nothing more than a wall. But then she lifts her wrists and taps one of her Kimoyo beads.

A hidden panel lifts straight up into the air, revealing a walkway into a dimly lit space beyond.

And when the girls get to the end of it and the automatic lights come on, Shuri doesn't stop K'Marah from letting her curse fly this time.

In front of them hovers a relatively large, but undeniably sleek . . . mode of transport. Faintly shimmery and obsidian in color, the vessel gives the appearance of a gargantuan panther midleap—head tucked, both sets of strong legs extended, and long, lithe body outstretched in a perfectly curved line. Just without the tail.

"The shape is for aerodynamics," the princess says, "because there are two modes." She taps one of her Kimoyo beads, and a pair of sleek wings extend out from the belly region.

"But what . . . is it?" K'Marah begins a slow walk around the perimeter of the thing, her awestruck gaze dancing over its lustrous surface, but not daring to touch it.

"It's how we're going to get out of here," Shuri replies. "There's more. Let me see your Kimoyo bracelet."

K'Marah holds her arm up in the air.

Shuri shakes her head. "No, silly. As in *give* it to me?"

"Oh . . ."

K'Marah does, then watches, baffled, as Shuri runs to the far side of the room and puts it on the floor before jogging back.

"Check it out . . ." Using her own bracelet, Shuri shifts and taps one bead, which makes the panther vessel rise higher into the air, and then when she rubs the top of a different bead, a whitish beam-looking thing shoots out from under the vessel and wraps around K'Marah's Kimoyo bracelet—which then comes flying at them.

"Aah!" the shorter girl screams, blocking her face.

"Sorry!" from Shuri. She reaches out and snatches the soaring jewelry from the air. The beam vanishes. "Still working out the remote kinks. It'll be smoother from the control panel inside. It's basically a tracking apparatus that utilizes the Kimoyo signal—and can fetch. I call it Kimoyo Capture."

"And when would you need something like that, exactly?" K'Marah asks, still shaken, as she takes her bracelet back and places it on her wrist. "Planning to lose your bracelet in the woods or something?"

Shuri shrugs. "You never know." She lowers the vessel back down. "Lastly, watch this . . ."

Shuri removes her Kimoyo card from a pocket, taps around on the screen a few times, then lifts the device to eye level and flicks the top edge of it forward as though tossing something from the card into the air.

And K'Marah gasps. Because right there before both her and Shuri's eyes, the vessel vanishes over the course of about ten seconds: from the outstretched front paws, up over the head, and down the body to the point where the tail would be. Now K'Marah *does* reach out, and as her hand connects with what looks like vaguely warped nothingness—"BAST, this is *amazing*, Shuri!" she says—a little heart-shaped bloom of some unexpected emotion bursts open inside the princess.

Why does Mother never react this way?

"I, umm . . ." And Shuri has to swipe at her eyes and clear her throat before she continues. "I've been working on something for T'Challa, and while doing some research on twenty-first-century superhero garb, I stumbled upon a secret organization in America called S.H.I.E.L.D. I went into their digital design archives looking for garment inspiration, and found the schematics for something they call a helicarrier. The flight technology was very impressive. So I . . . borrowed it. And made upgrades."

K'Marah spins to face Shuri, a look of stunned disbelief etched into her raised eyebrows. "Shuri, are you a *hacker*?"

"What?" Now the princess can't meet the other girl's eyes. "No, I . . . I mean, I put the details of the mirrored cloaking mechanism I added into the file as a form of payment—"

"You are totally a hacker!" K'Marah, beaming, bounds over to Shuri and wraps her in a tight hug. "I am *so* proud of you!"

"You're ridiculous, let me go."

K'Marah does with a chuckle.

"Anyway, as I was saying—" Shuri lifts her Kimoyo card again and flicks it back toward herself as though summoning something from a distance. The vessel comes back into view. "This is how we'll be getting where we're going." *Completely undetected, hopefully.*

"Fabulous!" K'Marah replies, bouncing on her toes. "What do you call it? You *have* given it a name, right?"

Shuri smiles. "This"—she gestures to the vessel—"is the *Panther Mobile.*"

"Uhh . . ."

Now she turns to K'Marah. Beaming. "You and I, future Dora, are going to Kenya."

MISSION LOG

WE MADE IT OUT—THAT IS *AFTER* MY "BEST FRIEND" LAUGHED IN MY FACE UPON HEARING ABOUT WHAT I CALL MY PERSONAL TRANSPORT VESSEL. SHE INSISTED THAT I CHANGE THE NAME OR SHE WOULDN'T BE STEPPING FOOT INSIDE IT (WE SETTLED ON THE *PREDATOR*).

But our skyward sailing certainly was not *smooth*.

Note: I must make some caliber and ballistic adjustments so that the vessel will make sharper turns, and the shifts in flight angle won't be so jolting. K'Marah experienced more nausea than I would've expected on our admittedly turbulent way through the forest.

Speaking of which: There is definitely something amiss in my beloved country. I fought hard to convince myself that my assertion above the plain was the truth—that the generals were gathered to discuss the final preparations for Challenge Day.

But our forced reroute—I couldn't risk flying *over* the plain, even while invisible, any more than we could've waltzed across it, especially with Okoye there (*informant!*)—revealed some other troubling oddities.

We went through the mechanized security forest on the southern border with Niganda, and I was able to use my Kimoyo beads to control the trees and create a wide enough path for us to pass through—up to a point.

Then we were attacked by a small grove. Of trees.

It shouldn't have been that surprising: The forest was designed to hide Wakanda from aerial view and to prevent intruders from getting in.

But I wasn't expecting the branches to begin lashing out and shooting laser beams at *us*. Especially since I should've been able to override them.

The first blow was like a slap on the *Panther Mobile*'s—excuse me, *Predator*'s—rear that shot us both forward and sideways. "Whoa!" was all I'd been able to manage. The laser caught us on the side. This time, the *Predator* herself spoke up: "*Warning, damage sustained to left flank.*"

Once I regained my bearings, I was able to dip, dodge, and maneuver around the arboreal swings coming at us, and even fire off some kill shots of my own (so glad they were mechanical), but once we were through that rough patch, I noticed some other . . . abnormalities.

For one, along our path, I had no problem distinguishing the natural trees from the mechanized ones—largely because a number of the natural trees were lacking their typical vibrancy. In fact, as we closed in on the border itself, we passed a cluster of trees that were glaringly dead. The trunks were the brooding dark gray of angry storm clouds, and the branches gnarled and leafless. And I can't be completely sure because we weren't close enough for a concrete observation, but it seemed the entire deceased copse was spotted covered with a strange yellow, like some giant had upchucked all over it. It was almost as though they were covered in mold spores . . . not unlike the soil around the dead heart-shaped herb plants.

Then once *through* the forest and officially in Nigandan airspace (without permission, oops), we passed over what looked like a small encampment about half a kilometer from the border.

Which I would've thought inconsequential had it not triggered an alarm. *"Warning: vessel detected,"* claimed the incongruously dispassionate mechanical voice. Which made my skin prickle as though covered in spiders.

Because being "spotted" should've been impossible. We were in *full* Invisi-mode, which not only involves the mirroring technology that mimics the appearance of the surroundings, but also a series of

Vibranium silencers that create a small vortex of soundlessness around the *Predator*, making its movement undetectable to the human ear.

We should've been invisible *and* inaudible.

Not only undetectable, but also untraceable.

Which now makes me wonder: What *was* that encampment, and who does it belong to? Wakanda or Niganda?

Or someone else? Are the Nigandans allies, or would they wish us harm?

And what is happening to the trees? Is it the same plague that is destroying the heart-shaped herb? Will it slowly eat away at our forests as well?

I *must* get to the bottom of all this.

Here's hoping my next log has more answers than questions.

9

TURBULENCE

And now Shuri can't relax. The flight to Kenya is approximately one hour and twenty-six minutes in duration—twenty-three of which have already elapsed—and the princess *should* be working on both acquiring permission to land, and finding someone to alert the queen of Shuri's intensely impromptu impending visit.

But every time she blinks, she sees the image that popped up on her security screen after the alert rang about the *Predator* being detected in flight: the head and shoulders of a man with his head tilted back and his hand against his brow, shielding his eyes. The picture is colorless and grainy (*note: Upgrade the vessel's security cameras*), but Shuri can see that he was wearing dark sunglasses and a solid-colored kufi cap on his head.

And if the tilt of his chin and the direct frontal shot of his face in the photo are any indication, there's a good chance this mystery man *did* see the *Predator* as it flew overhead.

But *how*?

T'Challa called shortly after they crossed the border, and although Shuri quickly deflected with a text message about being in the thick of a fabric test, he'll definitely call again. And she'll have to mention what she saw.

But what exactly will she say?

She peeks at the image of the man again—it's still glowing in the bottom-left corner of the console screen—and huffs.

"Will you sit *down*?" K'Marah grumbles from where she's reclined on one of the fold-down, fully adjustable beds in the open space behind the cockpit. She's "recovering" from the motion sickness she claims to have experienced on the ascent, but it hasn't escaped Shuri's notice that K's had a Kimoyo card in her hand since they reached ten thousand feet in altitude.

Said card chimes with an audible buzz of vibration, and K'Marah giggles in a very *un*–Dora Milaje–like manner.

Which sets off a different set of alarm bells in Shuri's head.

"K'Marah, who are you talking to?" she asks.

"Hmm?" K'Marah swipes and flicks and taps away . . . and then raises two fingers in what Shuri recognizes as the American hand gesture for *peace*, and snaps a photo of herself.

"WHO"—now the princess rises—"are you talking to, K'Marah? And what are you telling them?"

"Don't *loom*," the other girl says, sticking an arm out to prevent Shuri from getting too close. "If you *must* know, I'm talking to a friend."

"Named?"

"What difference does it make, Shuri? It's not like you *know* him."

Him. "So it's a boy?"

"Bast, you're worse than Okoye. AND Grandmother."

"This is serious, K'Marah! What if this *boy* is using the IP address of your Kimoyo card to track our geolocation? Does he know you're with me?"

K'Marah rolls her eyes, then shifts her focus back to her device. "Are you planning to be this way for the *entire* trip? If so, please take me home—"

The Kimoyo card slips from K'Marah's grasp as Shuri plucks it out of her hands.

"Excuse me!" the shorter girl cries, leaping to her feet.

Which makes Shuri take a step back. Yes, the height advantage is hers, but the princess is under no illusions about who would win *this* fight. Again. She almost hands the thing back just to avoid any escalation. But . . .

No. This is important. Tantamount to their safety—and that of Wakanda, in fact.

Which as a Dora in training, K'Marah should know.

So she stands up as straight as possible. "K'Marah, I need for you to tell me the truth. We are risking more than you know by going on this trip." (It's more than Shuri knows, too, but of course she doesn't say that.) "And I'm not referring solely to how *grounded* we will both be if my mother or your grandmother finds out about it. Not only are our lives at stake, the welfare of Wakanda is, too. As a rising Dora, you're supposed to be as dedicated to the security of our country as I am."

Now K'Marah huffs and crosses her arms. "You're such a killjoy," she says, turning her face away and dropping back down onto the bed.

"K'Marah—"

"If you *must* know, his name is Henny," K'Marah continues, unprodded. "We 'met' on the message thread of a PantherTube video about Krav Maga—"

"Krava *what*?"

"My word, you are hopeless." K'Marah shakes her head. "It's a form of mixed martial arts developed for the Israeli Defense Forces. Henny made a rather insightful comment about something in the video, and so I commented on his comment, and he commented back, and so I commen—"

"Okay, I get it," Shuri says. The *Predator* wobbles just the slightest bit, and Shuri peeks over her shoulder at the autopilot readings to make sure they're still on course. (They are. And the radar readings look good, too. They should be smooth sailing into Kenyan airspace within seventeen minutes or so.) "So you had a conversation. Then what?"

"Then nothing," K'Marah says with a shrug. "I haven't met him in person and don't really intend to. I only know he's Jabari because he told—"

"He's *Jabari*?! Are you out of your mind?"

"You know, to be first in line to the throne, you sure do sound prejudiced. The Jabari are Wakandan, too."

If the princess *could* turn red, she'd be the bright crimson of a lithium chloride flame. "That's . . . not what I meant." (Though of course it is. Could she have meant anything else?)

"Yeah, okay."

"And," Shuri says as a justification light bulb clicks on inside her mind, "let's not forget: They may be Wakandan, but the Jabari have chosen to cut themselves off from the rest of us. They don't submit to our rule." *They* are, *however, still permitted to challenge the sitting sovereign for the throne.* And Shuri supposes that *does* make it a good idea to be nice . . .

"Oh, boo-hoo."

A plume of rage balloons up inside the princess, and temporarily turns her vision the color of blood. "This is precisely why I *didn't* want to bring you! You're so flippant about everything!"

She watches the words land, punching not only the smugness but also the excitement right out of her friend's face. And instantly, Shuri wishes she could take them back.

K'Marah . . . crumples. "I'm sorry, okay?" she says, turning away. "It won't happen again."

Shuri's eyebrows pull together. There's a quaver in K'Marah's voice now that she wasn't expecting.

Then K'Marah sniffles and swipes at her eyes.

Now Shuri is *really* nervous. And not entirely sure of what to do. Her area of social expertise is with artificial intelligence, not crying best friends. "K'Marah? Are you okay?"

And the shorter girl sighs. Heavily. "I'm not sure I'm cut out for this, Shuri."

"What do you mean?"

"This Dora Milaje thing. Part of the reason I said yes to you was to get a break from all that. I want to be a Dora, yes. But I also want to be a kid. Who goes on fun adventures. With *friends*."

"Oh."

"I overheard some of them talking about me," K'Marah continues. "A few of the older trainees." And now she looks up at Shuri. "They said I'm 'too flippant.' Same way you just did. That I'm only there because of Grandmother's position. That she got me in. That part's not true: I worked and trained hard, and tested well. But what if they're only allowing me to *stay* because of who Grandmother is?"

Shuri doesn't immediately respond to that.

It's not like she doesn't understand where K'Marah is coming from. She opens her mouth to say something comforting—*I mean, I'm not exactly* princess *material, am I?*—but then there's a *BUMP* that jolts the *Predator* so intensely, both girls are knocked sideways.

"*Oof!*" Shuri exclaims.

K'Marah clutches her stomach and drops down

onto the edge of the fold-down bed. "Oof, indeed—"

There's another bump.

"Is that going to keep happening?" K'Marah says, now stretching back and draping an arm over her face. Shuri notices an ornate, charcoal-colored, glass-beaded bracelet beside K'Marah's Kimoyo one. Of course the glamour girl managed to add *something* ridiculous and impractical to her drab Merchant's apprentice getup.

Another bump.

Shuri completely loses her balance this time, and stumbles into the passenger cockpit chair. "It shouldn't be happening at all—" She breaks off to carefully make her way into the captain's seat.

And once she does, and her eyes alight on the weather radar screen, she's *very* glad to be sitting already.

They're not merely headed straight into a storm—one that was wholly absent when Shuri looked not ten minutes ago. It seems the storm is *trying* to engulf them.

Which can't be right.

With a slide, swipe, two-finger rotate motion, and *tap tap tap* on the navigation touchscreen, the princess makes some quick adjustments to the altitude level and flight path. It won't pull them completely out of the tempest, but they'll skirt the edge of what would be the most turbulent portion.

Then her gaze is pulled back to the weather radar screen . . . and she watches in combined awe and horror as the storm changes paths as well.

"This is not happening," Shuri mutters under her breath.

Another bump. "Get strapped in, K'Marah," the princess says as she does the same. "If you need to remain in a supine position, there are harness components that pull out from the sides of the bed."

K'Marah just groans.

"I'll do my best to dodge the worst parts, but things are definitely about to get . . . bouncy."

And bouncy they do get. In fact, the whole experience brings to mind some American thing called pinball that Shuri learned about in her Foreign Cultural Studies course just this previous quarter. Except *that* is a game, and *this* . . . certainly isn't.

Her Kimoyo beads light up, and a robotic, but oddly soothing, masculine voice fills the cabin: "T'Challa, aka Big Head Brother, is calling."

Shuri has zero intentions of answering, of course— he would totally *hear* the turbulence with his hypersensitive, heart-shaped-herb-enhanced auditory capabilities, and would no doubt have a cattish conniption—but knowing he's calling *does* shake a memory loose in the princess's mind.

T'Challa a few years back, sitting at a random table in the palace kitchen. Awestruck and chuckling and munching on plantain chips. "You girls are really something," he'd told her with a shake of his head. "I go to surprise the stunning apple of my eye, and almost lose my life as a result. Can you believe that?"

Shuri hadn't answered.

"I tell you one thing, baby sis," he'd gone on, "if you ever decide to fly over Kenya, brace yourself . . ."

That's when she slows the vessel to a complete stop, shifting into hover mode, and smacks the button on the dash that will make them fully visible and alert anyone in the surrounding area to the *Predator*'s full surrender.

Almost immediately, the storm begins to retreat on the weather radar screen, and the livid gray skies all around the girls and their high-tech, flying cat-ship dissipate.

Shuri exhales.

When the clouds right in front of the *Predator* part to reveal, not another plane, but a *person*, Shuri smiles. Apparently the girls won't have to find Shuri's contact: *She* just found them.

"Whoa," K'Marah says as she makes her way

forward and takes in the brown-skinned woman dressed in black, with white hair and flashing alabaster eyes, who has emerged in front of them.

Floating. In midair.

"Who is *that*?" K'Marah continues.

For a moment, Shuri doesn't say a word.

And when she does finally speak? It's barely above a whisper: "That," the princess says, "is Queen Ororo."

10

HEAT

At Ororo's instruction ("Wait, *Storm*? As in the X-Man . . . well, X-*Woman* Storm? You *know* her?" K'Marah said once she'd put two and two together), Shuri lands the *Predator* on the outskirts of a village a handful of kilometers inland from the city of Mombasa. By the time the girls disembark, Ororo is flanked by two very muscular men in T-shirts, tan shorts, and sandals. They've assumed a royal guard–like stance: feet planted marginally wider than shoulder width, hands clasped behind their backs with arm muscles flexed, chins slightly elevated.

"Okoye would lose her *mind* if a Dora Milaje showed up for duty dressed so casually!" K'Marah whispers as the girls approach their hostess. "Maybe I should request to transfer here . . ."

"Will you shush!"

"I'm just saying!"

"My dearest Shuri!" Ororo says once Shuri and K'Marah are within hearing distance. "What a pleasant surprise!" She spreads her arms and Shuri walks into them.

"Unbelievable," K'Marah gasps from behind.

This makes Ororo laugh. "And who might you be?" She releases Shuri and steps forward to extend a hand to K'Marah . . .

Who is frozen in place. Her eyes flick down and lock onto the Kenyan queen's extended hand, but she doesn't budge.

"You can shake it," Ororo says with a smirk. "Since you're a friend of my favorite princess, I won't electrocute you. This time."

A tinny squeak escapes K'Marah's throat, and everyone (except for her)—bodyguards on *chill* included—bursts into laughter.

"Ororo, this is my friend K'Marah—"

"Her *best* friend," K'Marah says, suddenly back to herself. "It is an honor to meet you, Ms. X-Woman

Lady Storm." She grabs Ororo's hand and gives it a firm pump.

"Ororo is fine, dear. And that's, uhh . . . quite a grip you have there."

"Oh!" K'Marah pulls her hand away. "Sorry!"

Shuri smiles to herself. She could get used to this bumbling idiot version of her "best friend."

"Come, we'll go into town." Ororo gestures for them to follow her. "Your aircraft will be safe here."

The girls comply—after Shuri puts the *Predator* back in Invisi-mode (can't be too careful)—and trail the white-haired queen and her guards to an open-topped truck propped up on overly large wheels. Once everyone's inside, the man in the driver's seat uses an actual *key* to crank the engine.

"Does this use *petrol*?" The incredulous question comes from Shuri this time.

They get underway, and again, Ororo laughs. "We don't all have *Vibranium* to power our cities and fuel our vehicles, you know."

"Wait, you know about Vibranium?" K'Marah sounds more panicked than Shuri realized possible.

"Ah, so the princess hasn't told you how we know each other," Ororo replies.

"I met Ororo through T'Challa," Shuri says. "She was—"

"Your king's first crush," Ororo says, looking as proud as a freshly preened peacock. "Don't tell him I told you, but I *rescued* T'Challa from a group of Vibranium-thirsty would-be colonizers when we were around your age."

(*If you let T'Challa tell it, he's the one who rescued* her, Shuri thinks.)

"Whoa . . ." K'Marah breathes, enamored anew.

"So, yes, I have full knowledge of Wakanda's store of the precious celestial resource. But you can trust that I would never do anything with the information that could bring harm to your beloved nation."

They bump along the dirt road in silence for a couple of minutes. Then a cluster of small man-made structures pokes its head above the horizon just as K'Marah says, "Is it toasty here, or is it just me?" before slumping down in her seat and shutting her eyes.

And Shuri must admit: She's not wrong. While the princess doesn't seem to be quite as impacted as her friend, it *is* hot. And much drier than she would've expected considering the location's proximity to the Indian Ocean.

They pull into the city proper as Ororo responds: "We have experienced quite the shift in our average temperatures over the past few ye—"

There's a loud ringing noise like an old-school fire alarm going off, and Shuri jumps. She and K'Marah exchange a nervous glance.

But then Ororo pulls out a heavy-looking device from a hidden thigh-pocket of her rather snug trousers. Speaking of which: She wonders what the weatherwoman's outfit is made of. It's clearly quite stretchy and seems to be moisture-wicking as well because good ol' Storm doesn't have a lick of sweat on her exposed arms, chest, or abdomen despite the blistering heat.

She makes a mental note to ask.

"This is Ororo," the incongruously blue-eyed woman says into the handheld item. So it's a phone. She winks at Shuri, but then her expression shifts and she shakes her head and pinches the bridge of her nose. "Again?" She sighs. "Fine. I'm coming." She hangs up, then puts a hand on the driver's shoulder. "Q, drop me at the greenhouse. This accursed heat wave has caused the atmospheric regulator to overheat, so I'll have to reset the spaces manually. Again."

"Would you like for us to accompany you?" Shuri says, jumping at the chance to assist her personal heroine. "I'm sure I can reset the regulator and, with the right tools, make some tweaks to the mechanism that will prevent it from overheating again."

"That's very kind of you, Princess, but I've got this one covered. Such is the beauty of being able to manipulate an ecosystem." She winks as the Jeep—that's what Shuri heard a guard call the automobile they're in—pulls to a stop in front of a low, glass edifice: The entrance is at the middle of a domed central building abutted by two longer sections that sit like arms extended out at its sides. Turning back to the driver, Ororo continues, "Deliver these wonderful young ladies to Yasha. She's at the station. I'll let her know they're coming."

She hops out.

"Girls, I'll be back with you shortly," Ororo says before shoving the door shut. "Lickety-split, like a lightning bolt." Then she gracefully spins away from them and jogs up the walkway to the building.

⬦⬦⬦⬦

Yasha is younger than Shuri expects: only a couple of years Shuri and K'Marah's senior.

She's also . . . rather grumpy.

"But *why* would Moe saddle me with *guests* when she knows I'm in the midst of *extremely urgent* research?" she grumbles while leading the two younger girls through the halls of a small brick building about a kilometer from where they left Ororo.

"Wow, she sounds just like *you*," K'Marah whispers to the princess.

"She does *not*," Shuri hisses in reply. "Who's *Moe*, do you think?"

"Why don't we ask?"

"She doesn't seem the type to look kindly on—"

"Excuse me, Yasha?" K'Marah practically shouts. "Who is this Moe you speak of?"

The Kenyan girl heaves an intensely exasperated huff and looks at the ceiling as if to say, *WHAT have I done to deserve such imbecility in my presence?* "M-O-E," she says, pronouncing the letters. "Mistress of the Elements?"

"Ah."

"Not to be a nuisance, but will we be permitted to sit soon?" K'Marah goes on, very much being a nuisance. She wipes her visibly damp brow, and her mismatched bracelets click against each other. "I'm feeling a bit faint."

Yasha forcefully exhales another puff of irritated breath. "Two more rights, and a left, and we'll have reached the dining hall. I've been instructed to provide you with sustenance, and then 'keep you company' until Moe is no longer occupied."

"Well, don't sound so excited . . ." Shuri says.

"I most certainly am *not* excited!"

"Not too quick on the uptake, either," K'Marah quips. Which draws a snort from Shuri.

"We'll be out of your hair soon, Yasha," the Wakandan princess says in an attempt to smooth things over with the Kenyan girl. "I know what it's like to be interrupted midtask and can understand your frustration."

The building they're in, as it turns out, is the Meteorological Research Center of Haipo, Kenya. And Yasha, at age fifteen, is the chief researcher. "My primary focus at this juncture is the effect of global climate change on East African nations, specifically this one," she tells Shuri and K'Marah over sumptuous servings of ugali and nyama choma.

"It is certainly *hot* here," Shuri says in between bites of food. "In fact . . . K'Marah, I wonder if you're experiencing heat exhaustion. We haven't exactly stayed hydrated."

"No idea," K'Marah replies. "But I'll admit: I'm astonished by just *how* much hotter it is here than back home. Yes, we're slightly closer to the equator. But man. Doesn't it seem *unnaturally* hot to you?"

"Where is 'home'?" Yasha asks.

"Wakan—OW!"

"Shhh, K'Marah," Shuri says through gritted teeth.

Yasha's fork stops halfway to her mouth. "You're from Wakanda?"

Now the princess glares at her guard-in-training. Then sighs. "Yes," she says, "we are."

To Shuri's shock, Yasha goes from prickly . . . to ice-cold. Flat mouth, narrowed eyes, the whole deal. "I see," she says. With undeniable bite behind the words.

Makes the princess feel as though she's jumped into a pool filled with shards of broken glass. "Why . . . do you say it like that?"

"Oh, no reason," Yasha replies with a shrug. "Though now I understand why you're so shocked by the heat here."

"You do?" This from K'Marah.

"Of course," the other girl goes on. "With all your advanced technology and your surely shiny climate-controlled buildings and homes, a drastic change in outdoor temperature must be little more than a blip on the radar for people like you."

Shuri can't think of a single word to say. "Well, I mean—"

"Many of your neighbors resent you, you know. Not we here in Kenya, obviously. Moe is *clearly* fond of your king." She forces a smile. "But there are . . . others. Who feel you Wakandans are self-centric and elitist."

Now K'Marah rolls her eyes. "How would *you* know how 'others' feel?"

"I am the Kenyan rep for the East African Climate Change Caucus," Yasha says. "Wakanda, of course, has no representative, but *all* of your surrounding nations—Niganda, Azania, Narobia, Canaan, Uganda—certainly do. As I mentioned, with the way you hoard resources that could benefit all, environmental concerns don't seem to be an issue for *you*, but they are for your neighbors."

"I—" Shuri begins to respond, but Yasha's mobile device buzzes on the table.

"Hello?" the older girl says, answering eagerly.

From the respite that slides down Yasha's face, smoothing her brows and cheeks, and dismantling the tension in her shoulders, Shuri knows their time with the cantankerous girl is up.

Which is a relief, yes . . . but also leaves the princess with the feeling of something vile laid over her skin. *Has* the climate changed markedly in Wakanda? Isn't this something she should know?

One of Shuri's Kimoyo beads illuminates to alert her to a new incoming message, so she removes her card from her pocket to read it in text instead of having the bead play it aloud.

It's from Priest Kufihli. "Fifty-eight percent and steadily spreading." Shuri gasps. Whatever's killing the herb hasn't slowed.

Two and a half days left.

Yasha ends her call. "Eat up," the Kenyan girl says, clearly thrilled to be almost free of her Wakandan burdens. "Moe—Ororo—is ready for you. And I need to return to my research."

11

STORM

There's no way to know for sure, but Shuri has a hunch Ororo has her and K'Marah delivered back to the greenhouse and brought inside so they get the chance to see good ole *M.O.E.* in action.

Without being trapped at the center of it, that is.

The girls can hear the *crack!* and *ba-BOOOOM!* of a thunderstorm as they follow one of the guards across the domed area at the center of the building. The greenhouse is significantly larger than it seems from the front, and the princess was incorrect about its presumed shape: There aren't merely *two* long arms attached to the central dome. There are five. The building is shaped like a half sun.

And as they approach the section at the center, Shuri can't help but smile: The hygrometer/thermometer combo gauge just outside the door indicates that the air within the room is dry and the temperature is too hot. But the princess is certain that's about to change. And she and K'Marah are going to witness it.

"Stay here at the observation window," the guard tells them (like they'd do anything different). "Queen Ororo has almost completed her task and will be right with you."

Then lightning flashes.

"Great Bast," K'Marah whispers, thunderstruck.

Within the greenhouse room before them, Ororo—*Storm*—is hovering midair with her arms outstretched and one leg bent slightly at the knee. An airborne ballerina wrapped in black. Her eyes are wide and bright as if the sun lives behind them, and her white hair billows and crackles around her, perfectly contrasted with the brown of her skin.

Shuri's not sure what plants are being grown in that particular room, but she watches, rapt, as Storm brings her hands toward each other in front of her and moves them in opposing circles like she's pedaling a bicycle with her arms. A wispy, white cloud forms between them, and when she's satisfied with it, Storm pulls her hands apart, then pushes them back together, spreads them wide, then brings them tight again . . . shaping, stretching, molding.

For the grand finale, she floats around the room, depositing the handmade cloud in long, wispy sweeps over the various lengths of plants. And by the time she's back on the ground and walking toward the door, the humidity streaks have gone from white to invisible.

Shuri takes another peek at the temperature and humidity measurements on the meter as Storm steps through the exit, definitely beaded with perspiration this time. Both readings are in the "ideal" zone now.

"You're like a goddess," K'Marah proclaims to Ororo as a guard passes the beautiful older woman a towel.

Ororo wipes the sweat from her brow. "A mutant, actually. But close enough." She grins at them. Now a hint of mischief flickers in her back-to-blue eyes. "Follow me."

She leads them down a corridor that runs alongside the greenhouse she just exited, and through a door that leads out back. They cross a short plain of dead grass that shushes underfoot and are soon climbing the porch stairs of a small cottage.

Shuri exhales with relief the moment they step inside: It's blissfully cool.

They've entered the kitchen. "Have a seat, loves," Ororo says. "I'll grab us some beverages."

The girls sit—well, K'Marah more *flops down*—at a wooden table positioned beneath a window that gives a view of the greenhouse complex a short distance away. Shuri thinks again of the plants inside it. Of the veritable magic Ororo just wrought on the *actual* atmosphere to keep those plants alive.

Why couldn't things be that simple for *her*? Walk into the Sacred Field, swirl the air around, and boom: Whatever's killing the herb would be instantly rooted out, and the plants would spring back to life right before her very eyes.

The gentle *thunk* of a glass being placed in front of the princess brings her back to reality. Ororo pulls out the third chair and lowers herself into it with more elegance than Shuri knew possible for such a basic act. Feeling bizarrely chastened by some inner voice, the princess pulls her shoulders back as discreetly as possible.

K'Marah, with much less discretion, bolts upright as if yanked by a string.

Ororo lifts her glass. "Drink up," she says before doing the same. "I know you both must be parched."

And she's right. So they do.

"Now," Ororo continues, setting her own glass down after an extended pull of the contents, "What can I do for you loves?"

"Is this your *house*?" K'Marah blurts, finally alert enough to take in the surroundings.

Shuri sighs and shakes her head. "Really, K'Marah?"

Ororo's eyes sparkle with delight as she fixes her gaze on K'Marah—who looks like she's about to combust beneath the force of the Mistress of the Elements' full attention. "Sometimes, yes," Ororo says. "Occasionally, it's nice to exist in a state of simplicity. People underestimate the value of *home* as a place of stability, where things subsist in a particular order and there's a rhythm your heart beats to." Now she turns to Shuri. "What has thrown your sense of home out of order, *dada*?"

Dada. Sister.

Despite the pulsing, sparking tangle of questions and worries in Shuri's head that seem to have grown multiple heads and legs, the princess exhales. "We are having some . . . vegetation issues," she says, risking a glance at K'Marah. It's not like she told the other girl exactly *why* she needed to come to Kenya. Does K'Marah even know about the herb and what it does? Is the princess about to blow some closely guarded royal secret?

Why does everything suddenly feel so tenuous?

She takes a deep breath. "There's this plant. As far as I know, it's unique to Wakanda. Has its origin in some sort of chemical reaction that suffused the space between the plant's cell walls and cell membranes with Vibranium."

Ororo nods. "The heart-shelled shrub, or some such, yes?"

"Heart-shaped herb," Shuri says. "But close enough."

"Ha! I get it!" K'Marah exclaims.

Shuri and Ororo both turn to her, expectant.

"You know, because earlier I called you a 'goddess' and you said 'close enough' and now Shuri is saying 'close enough' to you? Well played, Princess." She shoves Shuri's shoulder, and Shuri just puts her head in her hands.

"Well played, indeed," Ororo says without a hint of annoyance. (*How does she* do *it?* Shuri wonders.) "Continue if you will, please, Shuri."

"Well, the herb is dying."

Ororo's white brows lift, and something loosens in Shuri's chest. She clearly knows enough about the herb to recognize the gravity of the situation.

"Yes," Shuri says. "And fast. Just before we were brought back to you, I received a message from the head priest letting me know over half of the plants are dead."

"Whoa," K'Marah says.

"Indeed. Something is causing the Vibranium bonds to disintegrate, which irreparably damages the cell wall," Shuri continues as all the data she's collected thus far begins to scroll through her mind like the credits at the end of an American film. "Problem is, I can't seem to find any evidence of a foreign substance—other than the Vibranium—in or around the cells themselves. And I've tried every reparative measure I can think of. I've grafted the stalk of a dying herb to a living one, stimulated accelerated cell division, attempted to reestablish the Vibranium bond during mitosis—"

"Welp, you've totally lost *me*," K'Marah says with a yawn. "I'm taking a nap." And she puts her head down on the table.

Shuri shakes hers. "Are *you* following? I know I can get a bit carried away with the 'science-talk,' as T'Challa likes to call it . . ."

Ororo puts a reassuring hand on Shuri's forearm. "I do follow, love. Just not entirely clear on why you felt coming to see *me* would prove beneficial."

Another deep breath. "Well, that's the thing. I found records of an old . . . supposition, I guess you could call it. It purports that there were ancient Wakandans who learned to . . . do what you do." The princess nods her head in the direction of the greenhouse. "They would manipulate cumulonimbus clouds, and through this manipulation, shifted some celestial energies and created the path to Earth for the Vibranium meteorite."

"Huh." The corners of Ororo's mouth are pulled down in what reads to Shuri as *intrigue*, but she's still nervous about her next question: "Does that . . . sound like a thing that's possible, considering *your* abilities?"

"Anything is possible, my dear."

"You can say that again," comes K'Marah's muffled voice from where she's burrowed her face into her crossed arms on top of the table.

"Now, can I say *I've* used storm clouds to rearrange the cosmos and pull some otherworldly element from the sky? Sadly, no."

This makes Shuri smile.

"But I won't say it can't be done. Considering all the variables involved, it makes as much sense as any other explanation for cosmic phenomena that affect us here on Earth."

Now the princess has gone all starry-eyed.

"Don't talk nerdy to her, Ms. Ororo Storm," K'Marah says, lifting her head to prop her chin on her hand. "She'll fall in love with you."

"Oh, will you shut *up?*"

Storm laughs again, but it doesn't bring Shuri any joy this time. "I just need to figure out what's *wrong*," Shuri says to no one in particular. "I thought that maybe since Vibranium might've come to us through some storm cloud–controlled galactic gateway, perhaps *you* would know more about how that works. And if there was a way to use a similar mechanism to—ugh, I don't know!"

And she truly doesn't. In fact, the longer Shuri sits here in Ororo's sweet and simple little kitchen, the dumber she feels for coming. What did she think would happen? Ororo would kick into Storm mode, do some thunderhead sorcery to open a cosmic energy funnel, and suck the solution down, vacuum-style, from wherever it's waiting in the universe to be found?

Ororo's warm brown hand lands on Shuri's bare arm. Her nails are polished white. "While I'm sorry I don't have the solution you're seeking, Princess, I *can* assure you that no interdimensional space portals have opened recently, and nothing extraterrestrial has entered the Earth's atmosphere. Not within the past couple of weeks, at least." She winks.

Shuri sighs. "Well, thanks anyway."

At this, K'Marah huffs. "So much gloom and doom. Shuri, we've been to *one* place and spoken to *one* person. Surely an amazing scientist such as yourself has heard of a disproven theory and subsequent need of a new hypothesis . . ."

Shuri looks at K'Marah, affronted, yes. But also mildly impressed.

"Well?" the other girl goes on. "Pull your pretty little head out of the toilet and *think*. First idea didn't work. What's the revised one?"

Shuri's eyes narrow of their own accord, and part of her bottom lip finds its way in between her teeth.

"That's her *thinking face*, Ororo Storm," K'Marah whispers.

"Shush."

But K'Marah is right: It *is* her thinking face.

"You know, we've also experienced some vegetation shifts as of late. I don't know the forecast in Wakanda, but these global climate fluctuations have caused quite a bit of instability in *our* organic matter."

Which makes Shuri wonder . . . barring the small copse of dead trees the girls passed on their way out of the forest, Yasha was correct in her assumption that Wakanda doesn't seem too terribly affected by the environmental concerns plaguing other nations in the region. At least when it comes to the *organic* matter.

But we're all inhabiting the same Earth, Shuri thinks. *The only thing that makes Wakanda different is the presence of Vibranium . . .*

Then it clicks: The only plants experiencing problems are the ones infused with, or adjacent to, the bizarre meteoric mineral. Maybe the issue isn't with organic matter . . . but *inorganic.* Could ecological changes be affecting Wakanda's most valuable resource? Mutating it somehow? Is that also why she can't get it to bond with a new fabric for T'Challa's suit?

Shuri smiles as a new theory solidifies.

K'Marah sees and smiles, too. "Attagirl, Princess."

Shuri turns to Storm. "Ororo," she says with renewed enthusiasm, "do you know of anyone with extensive knowledge of celestial elements?"

TO BE CONTINUED.